Two little monkeys ran off to play.

Soon they had wandered far far away.

A bird found them crying a long way from home,

"Can I help you monkeys? You seem all alone."

"We've lost our mother. We want her back."

"Look! In the bushes. Whose tail is that?"

A lion's tail!

"We've lost our mother. We want her back."

"Look! In the tall reeds. Whose tail is that?"

A crocodile's tail!

"We've lost our mother. We want her back."

"Look! In the long grass. Whose tail is that?"

A zebra's tail!

NEIGH

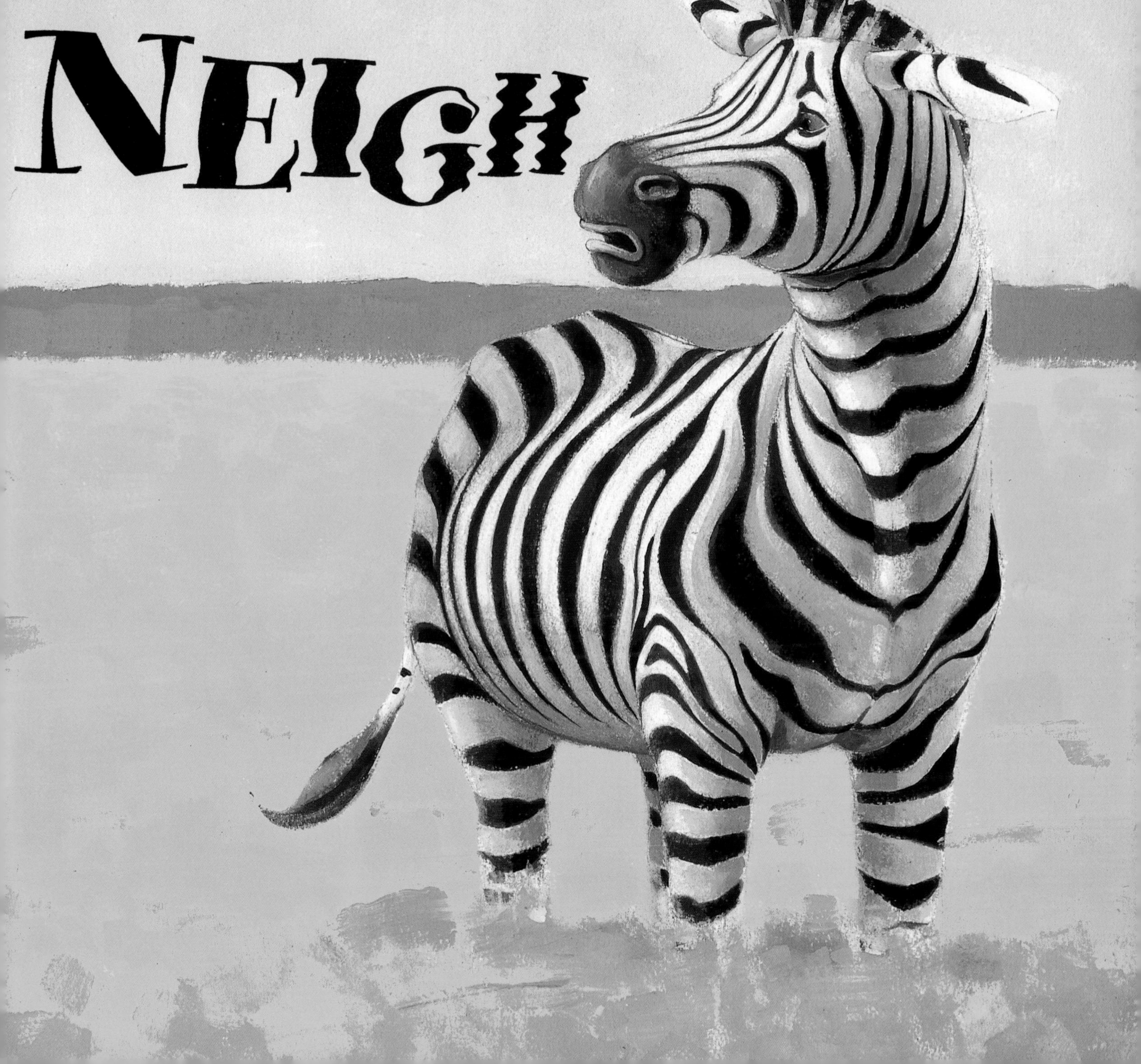

"We've lost our mother. We want her back."

"Look! By the big rock. Whose tail is that?"

An elephant's tail!

TRUMI

"We've lost our mother.

We want her back."

"Look! In the thick vines.

Whose tail is that?"

A snake's tail!

HISS

"We've lost our mother.

We want her back."

"Look! In the treetops.

Whose tail is that?"

A giraffe's tail!

MUNcH

"We've lost our mother. We want her back."

"Look! In the branches. Whose tail is that?"

A monkey's tail!

SCREECH

Now, three happy monkeys high up above,

Chitter and chatter with monkey love.

WHOSE TAIL IS THAT?

Written by Christine Nicholls

Illustrated by Danny Snell

Happy Cat Books

Dedication

To my mother, Elaine Alston Nicholls, who gave me my love of books when I was very young;
and to my father, Edward Maxwell (Max) Nicholls – C.N.

For both my mothers – D.S.

Danny Snell used acrylic paint on watercolour paper for the illustrations in this book.

HAPPY CAT BOOKS

Published by Happy Cat Books Ltd.,
Bradfield, Essex CO11 2UT, UK

This edition published 2002

First published by Working Title Press, 33 Balham Avenue, Kingswood, SA 5062, Australia

A CIP catalogue record for this book is available from the British Library

ISBN 1 903285 44 5

Printed in Singapore by Tien Wah Press (Pte) Ltd.